THE PARABLE OF
DIGGER'S MARVELOUS
MOLEBERRY PATCH

In Which the Windy Woods Campers Learn
the Biblical Value of Generosity

By Michael Waite
Illustrated by Sheila Lucas

A generous person will be blessed

proverbs 22:9

Dear Parents: *Read* Digger's Marvelous Moleberry Patch *aloud with your family. Talk about the story and ways you can be generous. Discuss Proverbs 22:9 and memorize it together. The verse will serve as a reminder of the Christian value of generosity.*

Be sure to look for these other Camp Windy Woods books and toys!

· Shelby the Magnificent
· Lady Bug Island
· Butterflies for Two

· Bartholomew Beaver and the Stupendous Splash
· Daisy Doddlepaws and the Windy Woods Treasure
· Camp Windy Woods Peel and Play

No time to dawdle about today! Digger's moleberries were nearly ripe and he had all sorts of weeding and watering to do. He put on his sun hat and gardening gloves, and hurried down to his berry patch at the Cottage-by-the-Lake.

"Tomorrow," he said to himself, dreamily. "Tomorrow they will be ready to pick, and Uncle Beardsley will help me bake moleberry tarts. Then we shall sit out in the garden and eat them!"

Just then Anthony Dormouse and Daisy Doddlepaws came marching up the path, toting their bows and arrows.

"Hullo, Digger!" said Daisy.

"Why weren't you at Archery today?" said Anthony. "We made our own targets. Mine was a Terriferous Gobblum." He held it up proudly.

"I had to tend to my moleberries," said Digger. "They're nearly ripe."

"They look very, very ripe," said Daisy. "As if they need to be eaten very soon." She sat down at the edge of the garden and sniffed at the berries longingly.

"Oh, dear... well..." said Digger. "I suppose it would be all right to pick just one or two for a little nibble, but I was planning to..."

Daisy gobbled down a half dozen berries in a flash, then licked her fingers happily. Anthony gooshed a handful between his paws to see if they would look disgusting. When they did, he licked them off.

They thanked Digger, and Daisy gave him a big sticky hug. Then they scurried off toward their cabins.

"Oh, dear," thought Digger, looking over the spots where the biggest berries used to be. "I had planned on making three platters of tarts. But I suppose two will be enough."

No sooner had he got back to his weeding than a happy rumble of chatter and giggles came floating up the trail. In a moment, Blossom Sweetpaws, Priscilla Prickletoes, and Barnaby Hopthistle came skipping round the corner. They were dressed in their swim suits and toting all sorts of flippers and snorkels and inflatable floaties.

"Howdy-do!" cheered Barnaby, tumbling into the garden. "We're going swimming. Want to come?"

Digger shook his head. "I would, but I have to tend my moleberries today. They're nearly ripe."

"They look delicious!" said Priscilla, eyeing them hungrily.

"Oh, yum!" cried Blossom, bouncing up and down on her roller skates. "Could we have some, Digger? Could we? Please, please, please?"

Digger looked down at his bushes doubtfully. There were barely enough moleberries for two platters of tarts. But if he didn't share his berries with his friends, he would feel positively awful.

"I suppose one or two won't hurt," he said, trying to sound like he meant it. "But it would be nice to save a few for..."

No one let poor Digger finish. They pounced on those fat red berries with such excitement it's a wonder the whole patch didn't get trampled!

They might well have gobbled up every last berry in the garden if Priscilla hadn't stopped them. She pulled Blossom away from the bushes by her tail and Barnaby by his ears.

They all smacked their lips and licked their paws and thanked Digger very much. Then they scampered off to the lake for a swim.

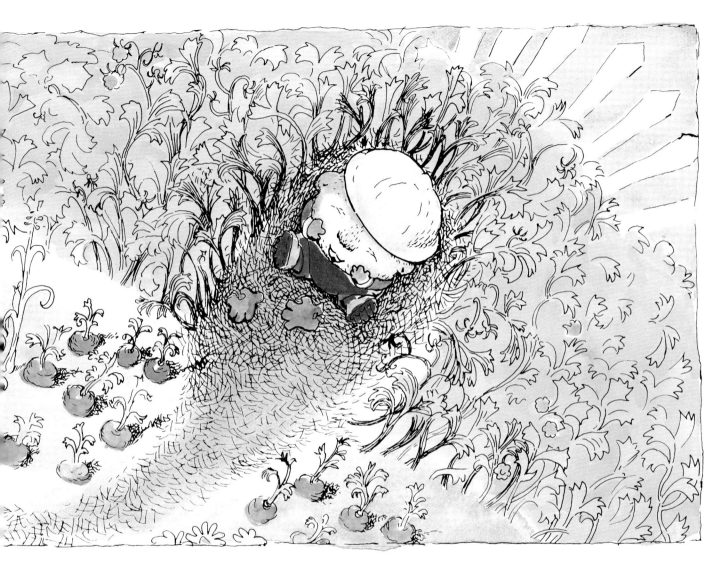

"Oh, fiddlesticks," moaned Digger, looking over his garden in despair. "Now I shall barely have enough moleberries for one platter of tarts." He sighed a moleish sigh, and pulled off his gloves. "But at least I made my friends happy."

Just then he heard a buzzing noise. It flew right past his ear and landed in the garden. He looked about the bushes and spotted a big shiny beetle.

"Oh no!" he cried. "It's a moleberry beetle! He'll ruin everything!"

"Scat!" he shouted, swatting at the bug with his hat. It buzzed angrily for a moment and flew away.

A few minutes later the beetle was back. And he'd brought four others with him.

"Shoo! Scat! Away!" shouted Digger, leaping about the garden, swinging his hat every-which-way.

"Fiddlesticks, fiddlesticks!" he cried. "Now I shall have to sit here all night long, watching my garden."

And that's exactly what he did.

He brought out a lantern and a broom for swatting beetles. Uncle Beardsley brought him his supper, but poor Digger barely had time to eat it. Each time he picked up his fork, a buzzy cloud of beetles raced into the garden, and Digger had to jump up and chase them away.

On and on it went, with poor Digger growing more and more weary as the yellow moon slipped across the sky. His eyes grew watery and sore, and his head was achey and full of buzzing noises, which got buzzier and buzzier, until at last he fell asleep.

When Digger woke up in the morning, he was surprised to find himself in his own cozy bunk in Tumbleroot Cabin.

"My moleberries!" he cried, and he jumped out of bed. He ran straight to the garden, expecting to find all the berries gone.

Instead, he found Uncle Beardsley sitting on the garden swing. He was holding the bug-broom and sipping a cup of cocoa.

"Why, good morning, Digger!" he said.

"Uncle Beardsley!" cried Digger. "You saved my moleberries from the beetles!"

"Not me," said Uncle Beardsley. "I just got here a short while ago."

Digger studied the berry bushes in wonder. Not a berry was missing.

"Go take a peek under the sunflowers," said Uncle Beardsley. "You had a whole Moleberry Patrol watching over your garden last night!"

And there, under the shade of the sunflowers, were all of Digger's friends fast asleep. They were still holding onto their bug-swatters. Their cheeks and paws were smudged with dirt.

"Shall we wake them up and thank them?" said Uncle Beardsley.

Digger smiled down at them for a moment, then said, "Not quite yet, if you don't mind. I'd like to give them a little surprise when they wake up... since they gave me such a wonderful surprise first."

"Oh!" said Uncle Beardsley. "What sort of surprise?"

"Come with me," said Digger, "and I'll show you."

While the moleberry tarts were still warm and steamy and full of sweet smell, Digger set them out under the sunflowers for the perfect Good Morning Present to all his friends.

Then he climbed onto the garden swing beside Uncle Beardsley and they shared the very last tart in the glad morning sunshine.

THE BERRY TRAIL

A Sharing Round
by Lucy Goosefeathers

Come with me on the berry trail,
Bring your pail,
Wag your tail,
Come with me on the berry trail,
We'll pick a bunch of berries!

We'll pick a bunch to gobble up,
Fill your cup,
Eat 'em up,
We'll pick a bunch to gobble up,
And a bucket full for sharing!

Chariot Books™ is an imprint of Chariot Family Publishing
Cook Communications, Colorado Springs, CO 80918
Cook Communications, Paris, Ontario
Kingsway Communications, Eastbourne, England

DIGGER'S MARVELOUS MOLEBERRY PATCH
© 1996 by Michael Waite for text and Sheila Lucas for illustrations

Cover design by Michael Waite
Cover illustration by Sheila Lucas
First printing, 1996
Printed in Canada
00 99 98 97 96   5 4 3 2 1